Paul Bunyan
and the
Winter of the Blue Snow

A Tall Tale Retold by Andy Gregg
Pictures by Carolyn R. Stich

River Road Publications, Inc.
Spring Lake, Michigan

ISBN: 0-938682-58-X

About the Author

Although Andy Gregg lives with his wife in Albuquerque, New Mexico, he has roots in the North Woods where Paul Bunyan accomplished some of his most amazing tasks. Born in Chippewa Falls, Wisconsin, Gregg was exposed to the rich lumbering history and stories of the region at an early age. In *Paul Bunyan and the Winter of the Blue Snow*, Gregg draws on his background to produce this humorous and imaginative tall tale. A photographer and writer, Gregg is the author of plays, fiction, and magazine articles, along with a more scholarly work, *New Mexico in the 19th Century*.

About the Illustrator

Carolyn R. Stich's lively pictures delightfully capture the fun in Gregg's tall tale of Paul Bunyan and Babe. Known for her attention to detail and expressive characterization, Stich has received recognition for her work throughout West Michigan. She studied commercial art and graphic design at the University of Tennessee in Chattanooga. Married and the mother of two, she resides in Holland, Michigan.

Acknowledgments

The author wishes to thank Dolores Beaudette, Chippewa Falls, Wisconsin, and the Chambers of Commerce of the cities of Hayward and Rhinelander, Wisconsin; Bemidji, Brainard, and Hibbing, Minnesota; and Grayling and Marinette, Michigan. I also wish to thank the officials at the Paul Bunyan Logging Camp, Eau Claire, Wisconsin, and the Empire in the Pines, Menomonie, Wisconsin.

Contents

People still talk about that strange, dreadful Winter of the Blue Snow in the North Woods. But not a person alive today remembers it.

Some say it's all a tall tale—how it began with an accident at a logging camp, and how Paul Bunyan, the great lumberjack, rescued everyone from dismal disaster. Actually, the whole truth of that terrible season has never been revealed until now.

This is what really happened. . .

A Cold Winter
on the
Big Onion River

It was cold that long-ago winter in the North Woods, so cold that pine trees froze, fell, and shattered into toothpicks. It was so cold that even big Paul worried about what might happen at his logging camp on the Big Onion River.

He sat on the hill and thoughtfully rubbed his jaw. As he rubbed, icicles flew from his beard like glittering frozen arrows. Nearby lumberjacks jumped, ducked, and ran from the icicle shower.

In the distance Paul could see Sourdough Sam and his men hard at work. Sam was a tall, skinny man with a mustache like a red squirrel's tail. He bossed the cookees who helped prepare the food. Some of the cookees hauled logs for the fires. Some dumped wheelbarrow loads of coffee into a steam locomotive used for boiling the lumberjacks' coffee.

Not too far from the locomotive was a hot spring where boiling water bubbled up from deep inside the earth. Sam and the cookees used the spring to boil pea soup. They used long-handled shovels to stir the soup, doing it ever so carefully so that they would not fall into their food. The loggers ate so much soup that the spring had to boil twenty-seven hours a day!

Paul's special soup peas were grown on farms in the East. Then the peas were loaded on ships which sailed around Florida to New Orleans. In New Orleans some of Paul's cookees put wheels under the ships. They used teams of oxen to pull their load north for more than a thousand miles to the logging camp.

On that cold winter day, Paul sat and worried and watched as Sam and the cookees dumped a boat load of peas into the hot spring. To flavor the soup they shoveled in two tubs of salt, four fields of onions, plenty of pepper, fat from a whole herd of hogs, and great gobs of stinky garlic. Sam looked up and watched Paul watching. He was worried too.

Both Sam and Paul knew that the axle grease had frozen on the boat wheels. That meant the wheels wouldn't move until spring. This would be the last batch of pea soup, and the loggers would get mighty hungry when the soup ran out.

8

Lumberjacks needed a lot of food. Monday through Saturday they woke when the cook pounded a big iron ladle on a tin pan and shouted, "Rise and shine, shanty-boys. It's daylight in the swamp!"

The cook always lied, for dawn was more than an hour away. The loggers crawled out of their narrow beds of straw mattresses and thick blankets anyway and trotted outside to wash up in cold water. Then the cook whacked the pan again and hollered, "Come and get it, or I'll throw it to the bears!"

The loggers crowded into the cook shanty, sat at long tables, and gobbled a quick breakfast of pancakes and sowbelly bacon. They called pancakes "stovelids," and washed them down with mugs of "swamp water" which was what they called their coffee.

After breakfast the lumberjacks shouldered their razor-sharp, double-edged axes and tramped into the deep pine forest. When there was enough light to tell a tree from a toe, they began to chop. After the tree fell, the 'jacks lopped off the branches and loaded the logs on sleighs. Oxen pulled the sleighs across the ice-crusted snow. Then 'jacks stacked the logs on the banks of frozen rivers to wait for a spring thaw.

As the morning wore on, the loggers listened for the cook to toot on his long tin horn called a gabriel. They welcomed the sound that called them back to camp for lunch. They stuffed down cornmeal bread, potatoes, and fried steaks made from what had been a lazy ox. They slurped pea soup, ate stewed prunes, and had more mugs of swamp water.

There was no talking, only chewing, slurping and burping. Then the loggers went back to work. The cook tooted the gabriel again at sundown. The tired loggers trudged back for a big supper of corned beef, potatoes, fresh-baked pies, and swamp water. After that they sat in the bunkhouse on a long split-log bench called a deacon's seat. They smoked pipes, mended mittens, sang songs, and told jokes and stories.

Sometimes loggers told stories about the fearsome critters that prowled the North Woods in those days. One of those critters was a hoop snake, a poisonous serpent that stuck its tail in its mouth and rolled through the forest. Loggers said an ax handle bitten by a hoop snake would swell as big as a telephone pole.

Another critter was the moskitto, a giant cross between a mosquito and a bumblebee. The moskitto had stingers at both ends, and each stinger could pump a pint of poison.

Still another critter was the large, spike-tailed Hodag. It looked ferocious, but ate only white bulldogs.

After the last story was told, the last pipe smoked, and the last song sung, the loggers crawled into their beds for a long night's sleep. That was how it usually was, but nature had a nasty surprise planned for the North Woods.

Frozen Fire

It was morning in Paul Bunyan's Onion River logging camp. Paul looked up at the snow clouds. They reminded him of giant lumps of curdled oatmeal. Paul worried they might fall. They could squash his workers as flat as Sourdough Sam's griddle. That griddle couldn't be any flatter.

The griddle had a history of its own. It was a heavy sheet of iron as big as a city block and was made by Paul himself. He had walked south three times to the railroad freight yards in Milwaukee. Each time he returned with a switch engine under each arm. He had piled the engines on the ground next to the cook shanty and shined the sun through his reading glasses to melt the iron into a hot puddle. After it cooled, loggers shoveled the dirt from under the new griddle to make space for a fire.

Now a fire blazed hotly under the griddle. A dozen cookees with slabs of bacon tied to their feet skated across the griddle to grease it. Then they poured pancake batter which had been tumbled in cement mixers onto the hot griddle. When the batter began to bubble, the cookees flipped the flapjacks with snow shovels.

To help the cookees, Paul reached down and plucked a maple tree from the ground. With a quick twist of his hands, he wrung sap from the tree and into a wheelbarrow so his loggers would have fresh syrup.

Johnny Inkslinger, the camp bookkeeper, saw this. He worked in a shack between the griddle and the hot spring. He saw all the work that everyone did in the camp. In a thick account book on a high desk, he wrote the amounts of every log cut, every pea dumped and every pancake poured. He even counted each feather pulled off every chicken, for those feathers would go into the lumberjacks' pillows.

Johnny wrote so much and so fast that he used a special pen. On the roof of the shack, a railroad water tank held ink that flowed through a hose to his pen. The ink, a mixture of blue dye and antifreeze never froze, so Johnny's pen always worked.

As Johnny scribbled his figures that day, the cookees began to serve breakfast. Some of them rollerskated between rows of tables a half-mile long and flung handfuls of eating tools on each plate. Others trotted beside the tables with fire engine pump wagons filled with coffee.

But then the trouble started. The coffee froze as it was poured and rattled like marbles into the mugs. The grease on the roller skates also froze, and the wheels screeched as they skidded across the plank floor of the cook shanty. There were crunching sounds as loggers chewed their coffee, and the snaps of frozen bacon breaking hammered everyone's ears.

Outside there was an even louder sound as Babe, Paul's giant pet ox, munched frozen hay. Babe measured forty-two ax handles and a plug of Star Chewing tobacco between the eyes. (That's what Paul claimed, although he couldn't be sure, because someone had taken a bite out of his plug of tobacco.)

Of course, Babe was always noisy. When he bellowed, flags flapped in St. Paul, and sailors on Lake Michigan thought they heard a fog horn. But when he ate frozen hay that day, it sounded like a thousand windows shattering.

Just when it seemed as if it could not get noisier, the bottom of the thermometer dropped out. The temperature fell with a crash that shook the whole camp.

Shot Gunderson, the camp foreman, thought they needed to know how cold it was and went to work on the problem. A wide man with a handlebar mustache and pockets full of tools, Shot could fix anything. He rigged three thermometers in a row. When it got too cold for one thermometer, the temperature continued on the next one. Shot, Paul, and the men watched as the temperature dropped out of the last one.

Although it only happened during that one weird winter, it was so cold that the fire froze. No one since has ever seen a frozen flame. It was yellow, like a hot fire, but so slick that the griddle slipped off it.

21

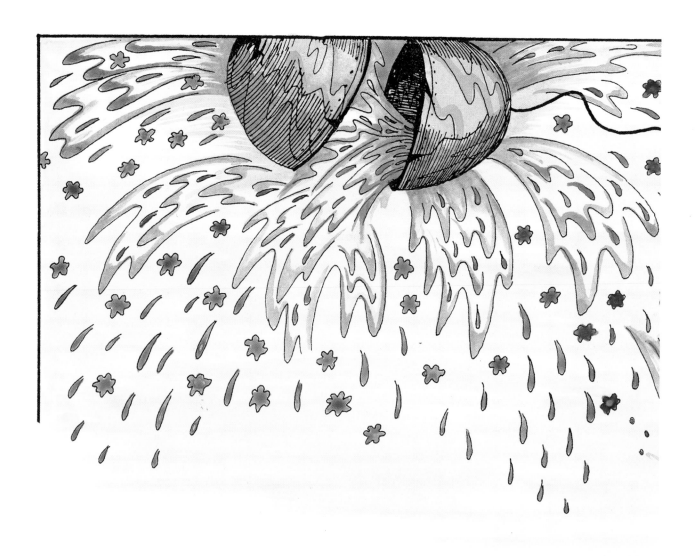

Cookees and pancakes tumbled in every direction. The griddle slid under Johnny Inkslinger's shack. Luckily, Johnny saw it coming and dove out of the door just before the griddle scooped up the shack and carried it away like a biscuit on a plate. The griddle came to a stop on top of the hot spring.

While everyone watched in amazement, the spring erupted with a loud WHOOMP! It spit pea soup high into the sky, along with the griddle and Johnny's shack.

Johnny's ink tank shot even higher, like a soaring rocket.
When it reached the clouds it exploded, coating them
with ink. Then it happened. Thick, heavy snowflakes
began to fall.

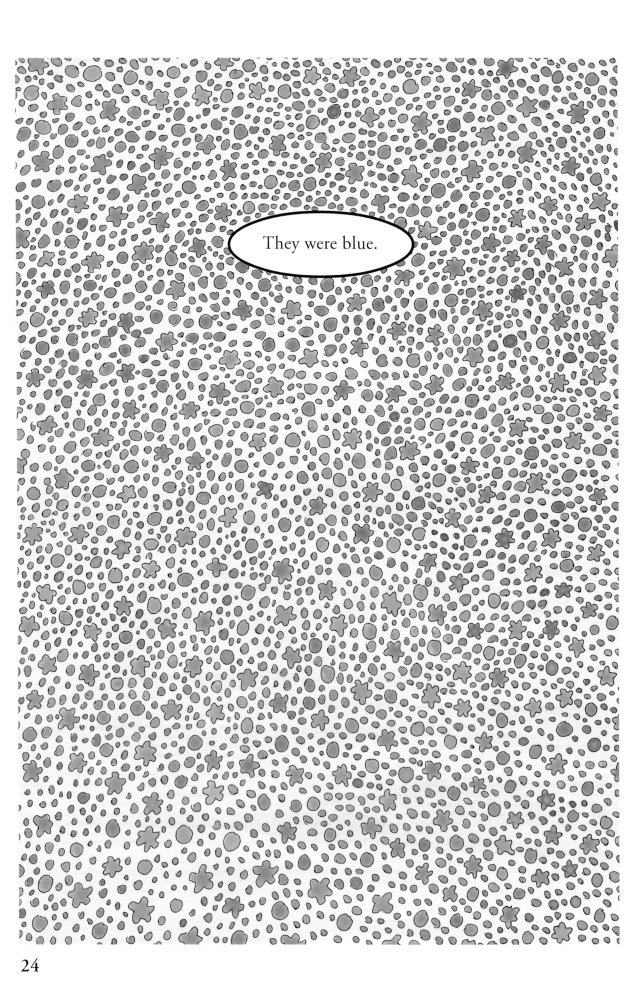

Trouble Everywhere

Through the day and through the night the blue snow fell in flakes as big as garbage can lids. First it buried the cook shanty and blacksmith shop. Then the snow buried the ox barns. When Big Ole the Swede, the camp blacksmith, woke up he saw frozen smoke oozing out of the wood stove. He slid out of bed, opened the door, and was knocked down by an avalanche of snow that pushed inside. He shouted, "Vake up, you lumberyacks, ay tank ve're snowed in!"

The loggers, still sleepy and complaining, crawled out of their beds. They grabbed their shovels and tunneled to the other buildings. Big Ole dug upward. When he reached the top of the bunkhouse, he exclaimed, "Yumpin' yimminy! There's no chiminey!" Snow covered the bunkhouse stovepipe.

Shot Gunderson climbed on top of the building and added pipe. As more snow fell, the chimney became as tall as a smokestack. Shot worked outside so much his whiskers were always frozen. This was very convenient. He tied loops of twine to his tools and hung them from the ends of his mustache.

No one else found anything convenient about the cold weather. Like bears and dogs that grow more fur to keep themselves warm in the winter, the men got shaggier every day. Their beards grew thick and long. The loggers wrapped their beards around their waists and tucked the ends into the tops of their boots to keep them from tangling in their saws.

As it grew colder, every sound froze in the air and flopped to the snow. Even the loggers' words froze in strange shapes. The loggers didn't know what the shapes meant, so nobody understood what anybody said.

The loggers almost starved to death because they couldn't hear Sourdough Sam dinging the pan or tooting the gabriel. The dings fell like plates, and the toots squirted out of the horn like long, cold ropes. Sam knew what to do, though. At lunch and supper times, he sent cookees on skis sliding through the woods while holding up signs with "TOOT" written on them.

Of course, the lumberjacks had almost nothing to eat because the fire was frozen. Luckily, the hot spring still boiled. The cookees made soup, but it froze in the bowls. Then the cookees began to put the soup spoons into the bowls first, and the loggers pulled out what looked like soupsicles. The soup changed in other ways. Now it was blue. Sourdough Sam said the soupsicles were made from blueberries, but the 'jacks were suspicious.

Everything was turning blue. The red and black Mackinaw coats became light and dark blue. Some red jay birds were frozen in the air before they could fly south, and they became blue jays. Even Babe, who had been pale pink, turned blue.

Besides "blueness," the terrible winter caused some other problems. One day Big Ole was in the woods when he suddenly felt stabbing pains in his toes. He limped and hopped back to camp, where he found other loggers sitting by the hot spring with their bare toes in the steam coming from the soup.

"It's them pesky frostbiters," Shot Gunderson explained. "They're plumb poison!" Frostbiters were small white worms with teeth so sharp they could bite through a thick leather boot. The critters slept all summer. In winter they hid underneath the snow and waited for a lumberjack to walk past. Then they jabbed their fangs into his toes. Sometimes they hung from trees, and when somebody walked underneath, the critters dropped down and bit ears, noses, or fingers that weren't covered with warm clothes.

Luckily, the steam from the soup saved the lumberjacks from the frostbiters. But the men faced problems even when they were in bed. The loggers slept under piles of blankets so thick they sometimes got lost when they woke up. A man could be crawling around under his covers and shouting "Help! Help!" but no one could hear him. Finally the 'jacks took logging chains to bed. When morning came they could follow the chain to find their way out.

With all that dangerous excitement going on, everybody but Paul had forgotten about the giant pancake griddle. It was still flipping through the air. Paul worried about where it might come down. If it landed in the middle of the ocean, it might sink a ship. If it hit a city, it could squash a few blocks full of buildings and people.

The fact is the griddle finally did come down. But it didn't sink a ship or squash buildings. Instead it came down a few hundred miles from the camp and changed Minnesota's geography. The griddle landed smack dab and kerplunk on top of the state's only mountain, Mount Itaska. The mountain was smashed into ten thousand pieces and scattered all over Minnesota.

Paul felt the earth shudder under his feet and he knew the griddle had landed. He just didn't know where. He hoped it hadn't caused any damage.

Help!

Paul noticed his loggers moved slower and slower. They wore so many layers of clothing they seemed as fat as snowmen. They walked so slowly their footprints waited for them to catch up and their shadows tried to push them ahead.

Paul felt sad and helpless. He was their boss, and he had to find a way to save them. If he couldn't, they'd be as frozen as the snowmen they resembled.

Then, in the blue distance, a small dark speck moved across the snow. As the speck came closer Paul saw it was a man on skis—a man who also looked like a snowman. His arms stuck straight out, and each thick mitten held a ski pole that he used to shove himself across the snow. His blue coat was darker than the snow, and his blue cap had a badge on the front.

Why, it's a mailman, Paul thought, as the man skied toward camp. The mailman stopped and slowly reached inside his coat. He got thinner as he pulled out an envelope as big as a pillow. On it was written:

To Paul Bunyan
Logging Camp on the Big Onion River
Somewhere in the North Woods
between Michigan and Minnesota

Big Ole and Shot Gunderson were so cold that when they ran to the mailman, they walked slowly. They took the envelope, opened it, and spread out a bed sheet with a message written on it.

Dear Mr. Bunyan, Please help us. Your griddle landed south of us, on what used to be Mount Itaska. If you remove your griddle, we will build a statue in your honor.

Mayor of Bemidji, Minnesota

Ahhh, thought Paul, now I know where my griddle landed.

Paul didn't say anything to the mailman, for he knew his frozen words would knock the mailman into the snow. Instead, Paul used sign language he'd learned from the Ojibwa Indians who lived in the North Woods. He signed, "I'm sure that Bemidji is a nice place, even if it has a strange name. Tell the mayor that I'll get the griddle, little mailman feller, as soon as I think of how in tarnation I can do it." Then he reached down, turned the mailman around, and gave him a gentle push that sent him sliding all the way back to Bemidji.

Suddenly Paul thought of a plan. He knew it would be even colder where he was going, so he buttoned his coat tightly. He put two hibernating bears over his ears for earmuffs.

Paul led Babe north to the shore of Lake Superior. They turned west at the city of Ashland and slogged through the snow past Duluth, Minnesota, to a deep hole filled with blue snow. The hole had been an iron mine. Beside it, some miners huddled together and tried to keep warm by passing around a lump of frozen fire.

Paul reached into the snow, felt around, and found the tracks of the Great Northern Railroad. In warmer weather, the railroad hauled the iron ore to ships at the port at Duluth. Using sign language, Paul asked the miners if he could take the railroad tracks. The miners nodded. Paul pulled up the rails and bent them into circles which he made into a chain to put around Babe's neck.

This had never happened to Babe before. He snorted suspiciously, and the steam from his nostrils fell like shovel loads of ice cubes. But Babe trusted Paul. The giant ox knew if he had to wear a chain, there must be an important reason.

Paul and Babe slogged all over Minnesota. Finally, Paul saw the edge of a half buried giant piece of iron.

He tied the free end of the train track chain around the griddle and whacked Babe on the back with the palm

of his hand. Babe grunted and snorted and tugged, but the griddle stayed stuck. Paul grabbed the chain and grunted and snorted and tugged. Then together they grunted and snorted and tugged, until that monstrous piece of iron finally shivered and moved an inch, and then a foot.

The griddle was loose, but Paul knew he and Babe still had a tough job ahead.

Going South

Babe looked to Paul, wondering which way to go. The big lumberjack wanted to go south, but he didn't know which direction that was, so he shrugged and motioned Babe to move forward. As the big blue ox pulled, the griddle plowed a wide, deep furrow behind them.

After an hour Paul saw a town. Babe stopped when Paul tugged on the chain. This must be Bemidji, Paul thought.

Sure enough it was, for people stood in the middle of Bemidji Avenue and waved to Paul and Babe. The griddle had landed south of town, so Paul now knew he had been going North. He shook the chain and Babe started pulling again straight toward town.

"Gee!" Paul shouted the command to turn left, a command that every load-pulling critter knows. But the word froze and plunged into the snow. Babe didn't hear it, and he didn't gee.

"Haw!" Paul shouted, but Babe didn't haw to the right either.

So Babe and Paul and the griddle plowed through the
middle of Bemidji as people ran like excited chickens.
Paul smiled as he went by. Sorry folks, he gestured, I'm
doing the best I can.

Outside of town, Paul jerked the chain and Babe turned in the opposite direction. Paul knew it had to be south. In Minneapolis they stopped while Paul decided which way to go. If they plowed straight south, they would go through the middle of some states, even through towns. So Paul decided to go along the states' borders.

With that they began to plow a furrow between Wisconsin and Minnesota and down between Illinois and Iowa toward the warm, sunny South.

Although it wasn't easy, Babe followed the twisting borders as Paul pulled on the chain to keep him geeing and hawing past St. Louis, Missouri, and Memphis, Tennessee.

The farther south the giant lumberjack and his ox went, the warmer it became. The ground thawed, and Babe moved faster. When they got to Baton Rouge in Louisiana, Paul ran and Babe's hooves flashed like blue blurs. The griddle had been sliding through so much dirt and over so many stones that the friction made the iron glow red hot.

At the edge of New Orleans, WHAMP! The overheated griddle burst into pieces. The griddle bits plowed through the fields and farms leaving furrows behind them and plopped into the Gulf of Mexico. Paul and Babe leaped high into the air to avoid the iron shards and splashed into the Gulf at the same time.

Splash? What sort of splash could one expect from a huge man like Paul and an ox as big as Babe? It was a giant splash, of course. Waves flooded the coast of Louisiana and made swamps of the lowlands. New Orleans almost sank.

The waves made by Paul and Babe did even more than that. They washed water up through the furrow made by the griddle, past nine states and into Minnesota. Before it stopped, the water reached the place where Mt. Itaska had been before the griddle crushed it. And, as Paul had hoped, the Gulf of Mexico water began to warm the land and air as it flowed north.

When Paul jumped out of the Gulf he was so worried about what might have happened to his loggers while he was gone that he started running toward camp. He left his earmuffs floating in the Gulf of Mexico. They woke and swam to shore.

Now there's nothing quite as mad as a wet bear awakened from his nap. The two bears growled, swatted each other and then jumped on Babe's back and rode like jockeys as the ox galloped after Paul. Babe, the bears and Paul all ran so fast they got to the Big Onion River before the warm water arrived. Paul stopped and stared in amazement.

The hot spring had frozen, and the lumberjacks had to chop out pieces of soup to eat. Their hair had grown so long that they looked like creeping haystacks with tasseled caps. The oxen, still hitched to the sleighs, had frozen, and the loggers pushed the stiff critters to slide the loads of logs over the snow.

When the men saw Paul, they wanted to smile, but they were afraid their faces would crack. They could only slowly wave and shout teeny "hoorays" that buried themselves in the blue snow. Soon they had more to cheer about.

Spring Comes to the North Woods

When warm air finally reached the camp, none of the loggers noticed it until they heard one tiny. . .

"TOOT."

It was the sound of the gabriel, almost too faint to hear. Everyone stared at the horn that leaned against the side of the cook shanty. The gabriel seemed as cold as it had been for weeks, but then, as they watched, a string of slushy sound oozed out.

"TOOTOOTOOTOOTOOTOOT."

The loggers cheered again.

"HOORAY!"

This time they heard their own muffled shout, so they yelled louder.

"HOORAY!"

Knowing what would happen next, Paul covered his ears with his hands and the loggers did the same.

The frozen noises and words suddenly thawed. The air filled with the sounds of chops, toots, sawing, crashes of falling trees, coffee being slurped, and all the words that were shouted and spoken and sung and whispered through that terrible winter.

At that moment spring arrived. Flowers popped through the snow. The oxen thawed and began to move and bellow and work and eat. The blue jays screeched in surprise and flapped south. After a few miles, they realized it was springtime and flew back. The hot spring began to boil again.

Before the loggers could eat pea soup, they had to get rid of their extra hair. Scissors and razors weren't sharp enough, so they stretched their beards out over logs and Shot Gunderson chopped off the beards with his ax. They shaved with their own razor-sharp axes. Next, Big Ole used tin snips to give them haircuts.

After the snow melted and the river thawed, the loggers used peavy poles and cant hooks to tumble logs into the water. Then they rode them downstream to join other log drives on the way to the sawmills.

At the end of the drive, and after many adventures with log jams that had to be untangled, Paul and his workers arrived in Chippewa Falls which had the biggest sawmill in the world. After Paul sold the logs, he paid his men for their winter's work.

The dirty loggers took baths in the horse watering troughs on Water Street, and then put on their best checkered shirts, blue denim pants, red sashes, high-top shoes, and new tasseled caps. Then they visited eating and drinking establishments with names like "The Bucket of Blood" or "The White Elephant." There they drank soda pop and sipped tea–at least that's what they told their wives and girlfriends when they got back to their homes and farms.

But the 'jacks also talked about the Winter of the Blue Snow, which everyone has heard of, but nobody alive today remembers, and how Paul Bunyan saved the North Woods from that terrible season.

What Really Happened

Today some people say these stories of Paul and Babe and the Winter of the Blue Snow are just tall tales. But it's true. All that really did happen! Here's the proof.

Remember the hoop snakes? They all froze in that weather. So did the moskittos, although some say that their smaller descendants still fly whining through the North Woods. Other fearsome critters also became extinct, and no one has ever missed them.

But not all those critters are gone. Frostbiters, for instance, still hound us. Some people might say there is no such thing as a frostbiter, but don't you believe them. Those critters love the cold, and they're still around. If you go out in freezing weather without mittens or a scarf, a frostbiter might bite you, although you will never see it.

What happened to the Great Northern Railroad? After Paul pulled up its tracks to make the chain, the railroad went out of business. You can travel all over the North Country, but you won't find the Great Northern Railroad there now.

Remember how Paul's griddle landed on Mount Itaska and smashed it into ten thousand pieces? Those pieces landed so hard they made holes in the ground. Later the holes filled with melted blue snow and became lakes. That's why Minnesota now calls itself "The Land of Ten Thousand Lakes."

Mt. Itaska is now Lake Itaska, and the river that flows from it is the Mississippi, which goes north and then south until it splits into branches at the delta at New Orleans and empties into the Gulf of Mexico.

Not only the red jays, but Babe, too, stayed blue after that winter. Now no one remembers Babe, the Pale Pink Ox. Everyone, of course, has heard of Babe, the Blue Ox.

The folks of Bemidji kept their promise and built big statues of Paul and Babe. The people of Brainard, Minnesota, thought it was a good idea and built even larger

statues of Paul and Babe. There are also statues in
Manistique and Oscoda, Michigan. There is even a statue
in California at the Sequoia National Park.

At Bemidji and Brainard, you can see some of the things Paul used, such as his ax, razor, toothbrush, and even his underwear.

There are other belongings of Paul's in lumbering museums in Wisconsin at Hayward and at Eau Claire, where you can visit one of his old logging camps.

At Rhinelander, in a glass case in that city's logging museum, there is even a fearsome critter. It is the one and only blue, spike-tailed ferocious Hodag.

So you see,
all of that
proves that every word
of this story
is
absolutely
true.